JEANNE-MARIE

COUNTS HER SHEEP

by

Françoise

CHARLES SCRIBNER'S SONS   **NEW YORK**

COPYRIGHT 1951 BY CHARLES SCRIBNER'S SONS
PRINTED IN THE UNITED STATES OF AMERICA

15 17 19 RD/C 20 18 16 14
ISBN 0-684-13175-7

Jeanne-Marie sits under
a tree.
She says to her white
sheep Patapon:
"Patapon, some day you
will have one little lamb.
Then we can sell the
wool and we'll buy
everything we want."

Patapon answers:

"Yes, I will have a little lamb.

1

We will live in the green field where the daisies are white and the sun shines all day long. We will grow wool for you, Jeanne-Marie."

"Patapon," says Jeanne-Marie, "maybe you will have two little lambs. Then we will have lots of wool and we'll go to the shoemaker and get new shoes."

Patapon answers:

"Yes, I will have two
little lambs.

2

But we will stay in the
green field where the
daisies are white and the
sun shines all day long.
We do not need new
shoes, Jeanne-Marie."

"Patapon," says Jeanne-Marie, "maybe you will have three little lambs. Then we will have lots of wool and we'll buy a red hat with a blue flower on the top."

Patapon answers:

"Yes, I will have three
little lambs.

3

But we will stay in the
green field where the
daisies are white and the
sun shines all day long.
We do not need a
hat with a blue flower
on the top."

"Patapon," says Jeanne-Marie, "maybe you will have four little lambs. Then we can go to the fair and ride on the merry-go-round. It is fun to ride on the merry-go-round, Patapon."

Patapon answers:

"Yes, I will have four
little lambs.

4

But we will stay in the
green field where the
daisies are white and the
sun shines all day long.
We do not need to ride
on the merry-go-round,
Jeanne-Marie."

"Patapon," says Jeanne-Marie, "maybe you will have five little lambs. Then we will buy a doll and a toy and a red balloon."

Patapon answers:

"Yes, I will have five
little lambs.

5

But we will stay in the
green field where the
daisies are white and the
sun shines all day long.
We do not need a doll
and a toy
and a red balloon,
Jeanne-Marie."

"Patapon," says Jeanne-Marie, "maybe you will have six little lambs. Then we will buy a small gray donkey. We will buy it from a little boy at the fair."

Patapon answers:

"Yes, I will have six little
lambs.

6

But we will stay in the
green field where the
daisies are white and the
sun shines all day long.
We do not need a small
gray donkey, Jeanne-
Marie."

"Patapon," says Jeanne-Marie, "maybe you will have seven little lambs.
Maybe eight
Maybe nine
Maybe ten
Maybe so many, so many that we will buy a little house with a blue room for me and a carpet for you, Patapon."

Patapon answers:

"Yes, I will have seven
little lambs.

7

But we will stay in the
green field where the
daisies are white and the
sun shines all day long.
We do not need a house
with a blue room and a
carpet, Jeanne-Marie."

And do you know what
happened?
Patapon had <u>one</u> little
lamb and a very small
one!
So Jeanne-Marie
could not buy any shoes
could not buy a red hat
could not go to the fair
could not buy a donkey
could not have any
house.
There was just enough
wool to knit a new pair
of socks for Jeanne-
Marie!

But Jeanne-Marie tried to look
very happy, anyway, for she
did not want Patapon to feel sad.
Patapon was so pleased
with her one little
Lamb!